KEELEY: BOOK THREE
KEELEY AND
THE MOUNTAIN
DEBORAH ELLIS

**Look for the other Keeley stories
in Our Canadian Girl**

Book One: The Girl from Turtle Mountain

Book Two: Keeley's Big Story

KEELEY: BOOK THREE

KEELEY AND THE MOUNTAIN

DEBORAH ELLIS

PENGUIN
CANADA

PENGUIN CANADA

Published by the Penguin Group

Penguin Group (Canada), 90 Eglinton Avenue East, Suite 700, Toronto, Ontario, Canada M4P 2Y3
(a division of Pearson Penguin Canada Inc.)

Penguin Group (USA) Inc., 375 Hudson Street, New York, New York 10014, U.S.A.
Penguin Books Ltd, 80 Strand, London WC2R 0RL, England
Penguin Ireland, 25 St Stephen's Green, Dublin 2, Ireland (a division of Penguin Books Ltd)
Penguin Group (Australia), 250 Camberwell Road, Camberwell, Victoria 3124, Australia
(a division of Pearson Australia Group Pty Ltd)
Penguin Books India Pvt Ltd, 11 Community Centre, Panchsheel Park, New Delhi – 110 017, India
Penguin Group (NZ), cnr Airborne and Rosedale Roads, Albany, Auckland 1310, New Zealand
(a division of Pearson New Zealand Ltd)
Penguin Books (South Africa) (Pty) Ltd, 24 Sturdee Avenue, Rosebank, Johannesburg 2196,
South Africa

Penguin Books Ltd, Registered Offices: 80 Strand, London WC2R 0RL, England

First published 2006

1 2 3 4 5 6 7 8 9 10   (WEB)

LIBRARY AND ARCHIVES CANADA CATALOGUING IN PUBLICATION

Ellis, Deborah, 1960–
Keeley and the mountain / Deborah Ellis.

(Our Canadian girl)
"Keeley : book three".
ISBN 0-14-305561-5

1. Frank (Alta.)—History—Landslide, 1903—Juvenile fiction.
I. Title. II. Series.

PS8559.L5494K444   2005   jC813'.54   C2005-905923-0

Visit the Penguin Group (Canada) website at **www.penguin.ca**

To Adam, Marcus, and Kaitlyn

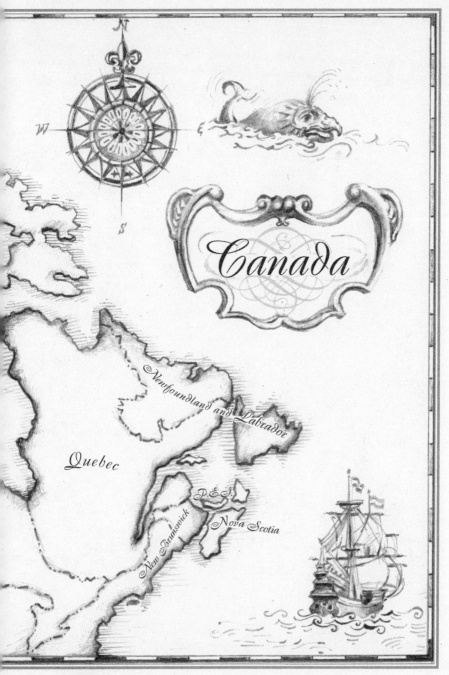

Canada

Newfoundland and Labrador

Quebec

P.E.I.

New Brunswick

Nova Scotia

Marks the location of the story

KEELEY'S STORY CONTINUES

KEELEY O'BRIEN IS TEN YEARS OLD and lives in the coal-mining town of Frank in the Crowsnest Pass, which is part of the Rocky Mountains. Although her mother died when she was seven, Keeley is very happy living in the boarding house with her father, who works in the mine and writes poetry. She has a best friend named Patricia, a part-time job at the newspaper, and enough interesting adults around her to make up for all the dull ones.

The town gets bigger every day, as more and more people from many different countries come to Frank to make money from coal. As Canada grows, so does its need for coal, to runs its factories and warm its homes. Coal mines are dug up and down the 60-mile length of the Crowsnest Pass. With the mines come shops, homes, schools, and newspapers, where Keeley especially wants to be. Women are moving into many jobs previously filled only by men, including newspaper reporting. The West is a big place, and there is room for a person to stretch and grow.

Keeley first arrived in Frank with her father on September 10, 1901—her birthday and the official birthday of the town. In the past year and a half, Keeley has grown along with the town ... but they are both still a little wild.

"*Only three mistakes in this article,*" Keeley said.

She passed the proofread article over to Mr. Matheson, so he could correct the type before the article was printed in the newspaper. Mr. Matheson was the editor of the Frank *Sentinel*. He was also the typesetter, printer, manager, and sole reporter.

"Your spelling is getting better," Keeley told him.

"I wish it were," Mr. Matheson said. "All week long, when you're not here to check, people come in to complain about my poor spelling. I wish you were fourteen instead of ten, so you could come to work every day, instead of just Saturday mornings."

"Maybe if you'd let me be a real reporter instead of just a spelling-checker, Pop would let me quit school now instead of waiting until I'm old and grey."

Mr. Matheson laughed at that. "If your Pop has his way, and he probably will, you will stay in school until you are completely grown up. We both know how he feels about children working."

"He doesn't think children should work in the coal mines," Keeley said. Her father was a poet, but he earned money as a coal miner in Frank. He had worked in other mines where children as young as Keeley worked deep below the ground. "He'd be fine with me working here every day, if I could be a reporter."

Mr. Matheson laughed again. "You can't dream and check spelling at the same time." He put another article in front of her. "Get back to work."

Keeley frowned as she looked down at the new story. She frowned even deeper when she realized it was about yet another speech made by the prime minister. If women ever got to vote, she'd vote for a prime minister who didn't talk so much.

She got back to work. To keep herself amused, she swung her legs back and forth. It wouldn't be so boring if she could at least look out the window, but she had to face away from it. Ever since a rather disastrous incident a year ago, when—through no fault of Keeley's (almost)—all the rows of little type letters went flying across the office, she had had to sit with her back to the window.

"It will help you to focus on your work," Mr. Matheson had told her.

It did help, although Keeley's mind was the sort that could distract itself easily.

"My legs are longer," she said. "A year ago, when I started working here, I could sit on this stool and swing my legs and not touch the floor. And now …"

Keeley brushed the soles of her shoes against the board floor as she swung her legs back and forth.

Mr. Matheson said nothing. Keeley knew this was his way of telling her to be quiet and work.

She concentrated again, and she managed to make it halfway through the article before boredom overtook her again.

"Nobody wants to read about the prime minister," Keeley muttered. "I could find better stories than this to report on."

Mr. Matheson threw up his hands. "All right, Keeley. Tell me. For a year now, you've been saying you should be a reporter. Just what would you report on?"

Keeley refused to give any sign she'd been caught off guard. "Bank robberies," she replied. "People want to read about bank robberies."

"And has there been a bank robbery in Frank in the last couple of days?"

"Well, if there was, you wouldn't be able to read about it in *this* newspaper," she replied. "The whole front page is taken up by the prime minister."

"I promise you, Keeley, if we ever have a bank robbery in this town, I will bump the prime minister off the front page."

"Unless he's the one who did it," Keeley said, so excited she hopped down from her stool. "Wouldn't that be a great story? 'Prime Minister Holds Up Bank.'"

"I knew I shouldn't have voted for him," a voice behind Keeley said.

She turned around. There were her father and Violet, their friend from the boarding house.

"Mr. O'Brien, kindly tell your daughter that the Frank *Sentinel* cannot print a story about a bank robbery unless there actually is a bank robbery." Mr. Matheson pretended to sound stern, but he greeted Keeley's father and Violet with a friendly smile. He didn't shake their hands, though, as his own were covered in printer's ink.

"My daughter should be concentrating on her work, and, when she's not thinking of that, on the spelling bee this afternoon."

"Oh, don't worry about that," Keeley said. "I'll be the Spelling Champion of the Crowsnest Pass again."

"Two years in a row?" Violet asked.

"Twenty years in a row! I'll get the five-dollar prize every year, and Cora Hind will write about me in all the big newspapers and I'll be famous." Cora Hind was a reporter. Keeley wanted to be just like her when she grew up.

"Pride goeth ...," Mr. Matheson began.

"Pride goeth before the fall, I know," Keeley said. "Mrs. Greer has been quoting that to me all week." Mrs. Greer ran the boarding house where Keeley, her father, and Violet lived. When Keeley had first moved to Frank, a year and a half before, she had wanted to live in one of the little houses the coal company had built for the miners and their families, but her father didn't have enough money. Now, Keeley felt right at home in the boarding house.

"You didn't study as much this time," her father reminded her.

"The words are all up here." Keeley tapped her forehead.

"Which means you have room in your stomach for lunch," Violet said, lifting the picnic basket she was carrying onto the counter. "There's plenty here for you too, Harry," she said to Mr. Matheson.

While Keeley's boss washed the ink off his hands, Violet laid out the sandwiches.

"I saw Lillian pressing your blue dress," Violet said. Lillian was Mrs. Greer's assistant. "Is that what you're going to wear to the spelling bee?"

Keeley nodded. "Mrs. Greer had to let it out at the sides and the bottom. She said, 'You *would* pick this week to grow!'"

"She's hoping you'll learn to sew," her father said.

"Too much sitting still," Keeley replied. She took a bite out of her sandwich, chewed quickly, and swallowed. "I like to move around and have adventures and report on exciting crimes and have lots of admirers."

"There's one of your admirers now," Mr. Matheson said, towelling off his hands and nodding at the window.

Keeley spun around. There was Peter, the boy from her class who had been her biggest enemy since the day she came to Frank. His face was pressed up against the glass. His tongue was out, and his hands wiggled in his ears.

In a flash, Keeley was after him. Out the door and down the street, Keeley chased her classmate through the groups of Saturday shoppers that crowded the wooden sidewalks of Dominion Street. A few times, she almost grabbed him, but Peter had a good head start, and he made the most of it.

Finally, Keeley gave up. She had to be content with yelling at him. "I beat you in last year's spelling bee," she bellowed, "and I'll beat you again today!"

"Pride goeth before the fall," a lady said as she walked by.

Keeley just rolled her eyes.

"There's one of your admirers now," Mr. Matheson said, towelling off his hands and nodding at the window.

CHAPTER N°2

"More honey cake, Keeley?" Mable asked.

Keeley always had room for more honey cake, made with the honey from Granny Mable's own bees, but she shook her head.

"I've just remembered how miserable I am."

It had been easy to forget, for a little while. Dinner at her best friend Patricia's house, with Patricia's two grandmothers, Mable and Ethel, was always a happy time.

Dinners at the boarding house were fun, too. Mrs. Greer always had newcomers passing through, with new stories to tell. But at the boarding house, Keeley was considered a child, someone to speak only if directly spoken to.

At Mable and Ethel's house, children could speak, disagree, and change the topic. The only thing she and Patricia were discouraged from doing—apart from the usual list of things that were plain bad manners, which they were too old to do anyway—was raise their voices.

"A loud voice doesn't make up for a weak argument," Ethel was fond of saying.

"The best cure for misery is another piece of honey cake," Mable said, plonking a slice in front of Keeley.

"I thought the best cure for misery was a good long walk," Patricia said, "or chopping wood."

"Or a dip in the river or climbing a tree," Ethel added. "There are many best cures for misery."

"What about shame?" Keeley asked, with her mouth full of cake.

"Depends on the kind of shame," Ethel said. "If you kill somebody out of meanness, you should feel shame. It might keep you from killing again. Did you kill anybody we should know about?"

In spite of herself, Keeley laughed. "No, but I did goof up at the spelling bee. The first word, too!"

"Anybody could mix up the *i* and the *a* in *giant*," Mable said, pouring more cider into Keeley's glass. "There's no shame in that."

"At least Cora Hind wasn't there this year to see me fail," Keeley said. Cora Hind had been a judge last year and had given Keeley her prize. "But I told everybody I would win. People will ask me what happened."

"Hold your head high, look them in the eye, and say, 'I goofed,'" said Ethel. "If you go around looking ashamed, they'll just quote pride scriptures at you again."

Then Patricia changed the subject. "What do you think Anne Boleyn ate before she had her head cut off?" Patricia read all the time, and now she was reading about King Henry the Eighth and all his unfortunate wives. This led to a discussion about whether it would be better to have a wonderful last meal or a terrible one.

"If my last meal were chicken livers, I'd welcome the axe," Mable said.

The discussion was so interesting, it lasted all through the dishes.

"Can you stay over?" Patricia asked. It was something Keeley often did, especially since her father worked the night shift.

"Mrs. Greer is expecting me back at the boarding house, so I'd better go."

"I'll walk you home," Ethel said. She fetched her coat, and Keeley got hers from the peg by the door.

"Peter will be impossible after this," Patricia said. "We'll have to figure out something really great to make things right again."

Keeley liked how Patricia said "we." She also liked how happy Patricia looked at the prospect of hatching a new scheme.

Granny Ethel carved strange-looking statues out of thick logs and tree stumps. They were all over the yard. The full moon made them look even weirder. Ethel got her axe from where she had left it sticking out of the head of what could be a mountain goat or maybe a fish. She hadn't finished carving it yet.

Granny Ethel carried her axe the way some ladies carried a purse. "Might try carving in the moonlight," she said. "Might prove interesting. Everything looks different in the moonlight." She shivered. "It sure has gotten cold all of a sudden. It's been so warm all month."

Keeley felt the cold, too. April so far had been unusually warm, but tonight it felt like the dead of winter again.

Keeley travelled from Patricia's house to the boarding house so often, she could probably do it blindfolded. She really didn't need Ethel to come with her. It was nice to have the company, though. Ethel was the sort of adult who didn't ask children stupid questions.

They passed through the meadow, stopping to watch a family of deer munching grass in the moonlight. After another patch of woods, they came to Andy Grissick's camp.

"He'll be cold in that tent tonight," Keeley said.

"That old trapper? If he can survive living in the tent in January, he can stand it in April. Hey, Andy, are you awake?"

"A full moon brings out all the fools," a voice growled back. "I suppose you want some coffee."

Ethel and Keeley joined Andy at his campfire. Keeley had been afraid of Andy's grizzled old face when she had first met him, but that didn't last long. Now, she'd rather listen to his stories than do just about anything.

However, there was no story tonight. He and Ethel got into a spirited debate about whether the Irish immigrants had bought leprechauns with them to Canada and, if so, where in the Rockies would be the best place to find them.

"I'd better go," Keeley said after a while. She was getting tired and cold.

"Yes, go on home," Ethel said. "Remember to hold your head high, no matter what people say.

There is nothing more powerful than a woman who can't be shamed."

That's all very well if you carry an axe, Keeley thought as she said goodnight. *Although if I start carrying an axe, people will just tell me to put it down before I hurt myself.*

It seemed to Keeley that every time she walked from Patricia's house to the boarding house, there were more new homes and more tents set up. Turtle Mountain was full of coal, and people kept coming to Frank, planning on getting rich.

"We don't even have to mine it any more," one of the miners had said at breakfast a few days before. "The coal jumps right out of the mountain and into our coal cart for Charlie to take away." Charlie was Keeley's favourite mine horse, who pulled the carts full of coal out of the mountain.

Some of the new miners were huddled around cook fires, trying to keep warm. They sang songs in languages Keeley couldn't name.

Everybody comes to Frank, she thought. It was an exciting place to live, even if there weren't a lot of bank robberies.

Keeley entered the boarding house through the kitchen door. Mrs. Greer and Lillian were just finishing up for the night.

"There's some hot water in the kettle," Mrs. Greer said to Keeley. "Fix yourself a hot drink. I can't believe how cold it's gotten all of a sudden."

Keeley put her coat on the back of a kitchen chair. She got out a mug, put a bit of cider in the bottom, and filled the rest of the cup with hot water. It warmed her insides. A plate of molasses cookies was on the table. She was wondering if she should ask for one, but Mrs. Greer beat her to it and passed her the plate.

Lillian hung the last of the pots on the rack and took off her apron. "What a long day," she said, sitting down.

"Are you sure you wouldn't rather sleep here tonight?" Mrs. Greer asked. "I know you don't live far, but it's so late, and you're clearly tired."

"I've never stayed away from my family before," Lillian replied.

"At sixteen years of age, it's time you did," said Mrs. Greer.

"She could sleep in Pop's bed," Keeley offered. "He's at the mine."

"Do you really think I should?" Lillian asked.

"I'll send Ralph over to tell your family," Mrs. Greer said. Ralph was her handyman.

While the two women made arrangements, Keeley grabbed another cookie.

"Take that up with you," Mrs. Greer said. "Bring the mug down in the morning."

Keeley got up and started out of the kitchen.

"And Keeley," Mrs. Greer began.

Keeley stopped and faced her.

"If the worst thing that ever happens to you is that you make a mistake in the spelling bee, you'll be a lucky woman."

It was better than the pride quote. Keeley said goodnight and climbed the stairs to the little room at the top of the house that she shared with her father. She thought about knocking on Violet's door, to say goodnight, but she remembered that Violet would still be performing her songs and dances in the saloon.

While Keeley finished her drink and cookie, she looked at her mother's paintings that hung on the walls of the little room. Her mother had been an artist before she died, and she had painted beautiful scenes of nature and people. When Keeley looked at them, it made her feel as if her mother were still with her. She sighed and got into her nightgown.

Lillian soon joined Keeley and they put the light out.

Keeley's bed was built right into a narrow space beside the dormer window. As she did every night, Keeley knelt on her bed and looked out the window at Turtle Mountain where her father was working. She waved at him, although she knew he couldn't see her. At this time of the night, he was deep inside the mine. He got a lunch break at 4 A.M. He usually went outside the mine to sit on the tipple and breathe fresh air while he ate his sandwich. If Keeley woke up in the middle of the night, she'd wave again, just in case it was his lunchtime.

This had been a long day. Keeley got under her covers, said a final goodnight to Lillian, and was soon sound asleep.

CHAPTER N° 3

Keeley landed on the floor with a thud.

Something had picked her up and thrown her with the force of a monster. She wasn't fully awake until she bounced off her bedroom wall, landing brutally on the floor.

"Hey!" she tried to call out, but her voice was completely overtaken by the loudest sound she had ever heard. It was a roar and a hiss and it was coming straight for her.

Hands reached for her. Keeley recognized Lillian, who pulled her to her feet and out of the room. The boarding house shook, knocking them back and forth as they ran down the stairs. Other tenants were heading down, too, all in their nightclothes. A big man pushed Keeley and Lillian out of his way as he ran.

Violet helped them to their feet. Keeley couldn't see her clearly, because the house was in darkness, but she could smell Violet's flowery perfume. She clung to her friend until they reached the main floor.

"The boarding house is falling down!" the big man was yelling. He grabbed Mrs. Greer who was rushing about with a lantern. "I want my money back! I paid you in advance and I want my money back!"

Mrs. Greer slapped him hard across the face. He calmed down and let her go.

"Wait here," Violet told Keeley, putting her into a chair in the parlour. She had to shout to be heard over the roar. "I'll try to find out what's going on."

Not even for Violet would Keeley sit still. She got out of her chair and opened the front door.

Rocks were raining down on Frank like hail from Hell. Wind and cold and dust blasted at Keeley.

A grown-up behind her shut the door. "Don't be so foolish," he said.

To Keeley, that was a dare. Something was actually happening, perhaps something even better than a bank robbery, and there was no way she was going to miss it.

She slipped through the frightened adults standing together in groups like cows during a rainstorm. Her shoes were in the kitchen. She pulled them on over her bare feet, grabbed her coat off the back of the chair, and headed out the back door.

The wind knocked her right off her feet. She landed hard on the ground, hitting her head against the side of the boarding house.

Maybe this wasn't such a good idea, she said to herself. It was only the thought of being cooped up with all those adults that kept her outside.

Step by step, bent over, she made her way out of the yard and onto Dominion Street.

The wind knocked her
right off her feet.

Things blew past her at such speed, she couldn't tell if they were stop signs, sticks, or bits off rooftops.

It's a tornado, she thought. *We'll be blown down to Oz. The Wizard of Oz* was one of the few books Patricia had persuaded Keeley to read.

A few other people had come into the street. The darkness was so thick with dust, Keeley almost bumped right into people before she saw them.

"It's the end of the world!" a man cried out, running without seeming to know why. "It's Judgment Day!" He grabbed hold of Keeley's shoulders and shook her as he yelled.

Keeley wished she could reach up and slap him the way Mrs. Greer had slapped the man in the boarding house. The man didn't stick around though. He let go of her and ran off, shouting as he went.

Keeley realized then that the terrible noise had quieted down. The wind had stopped too. Whatever had happened, it was all over.

"It's not the end of the world after all," Keeley said with a laugh. Her laugh ended in a cough, as the dust got into her throat. "It's just a bit of excitement that most people were too scared to see!"

But *she* had seen it! This could be the story she could finally write for the newspaper! Now, if there could only be a bank robbery on top of it, she'd be as famous a newspaper woman as Cora Hind. Her father would be so proud!

She decided to keep heading down Dominion Street, just in case there was a robbery happening. She didn't get far, though. She was walked right into by a woman in a nightgown. The woman was moaning.

"Everything is fine," Keeley told her. "The world is still here. It didn't end."

The woman just moaned again. Even in the early morning darkness, what Keeley saw in the stranger's face scared her. She took her coat off and put it around the woman's shoulders. The woman didn't seem to notice.

"Let's go where it's warm," Keeley said, taking the woman's arm.

The swirling dust was thick like fog. Keeley was not entirely sure where the boarding house was. She saw some lights and headed in that direction. The saloon had opened up. Keeley pushed open the swinging door and put the woman into a seat near the stove.

The saloonkeeper brought a small glass of whiskey to their table. "Get your mother to drink this," he said. "She's in shock, and no wonder."

"She's not my mother," Keeley said. "I don't know who she is. We bumped into each other in the street."

The saloonkeeper nodded at the whiskey glass, then looked harder at Keeley. "Young lady, do you realize that you've been hurt?"

He took his bar towel and wiped Keeley's face. She was astonished at the blood he wiped away.

"I don't feel anything," she said.

"You're in shock, too," he said. He tilted her head toward the light. "You'll bleed for a while, but don't worry about it. Head wounds bleed a lot. I see a lot of them."

"I know," Keeley said, pressing the towel against her head where he showed her. "My friend and I see you break up lots of fights."

He looked at her again. "Your hair is usually in pigtails?" She nodded. "You're that girl I'm always chasing away from my window?" Keeley nodded again. "And now here you sit in my saloon." They smiled at each other. "Get her to drink that whiskey," he said. He fetched a blanket for the woman so Keeley could have her coat back.

Keeley put the woman's hand around the whiskey glass. The woman just sat there.

"At least you're warm now," Keeley said to her. "It will be light soon. You'll be able to find your way home then."

Keeley sat with the woman for a while, watching the bar fill up. As the warmth of the woodstove helped her relax, she started feeling pain from the wound on her head. At least the bleeding seemed to be slowing.

The people coming into the bar were not acting as though an exciting adventure had just happened. Their faces were grave, and they spoke in low tones. They gulped down their drinks like they were trying to shake away something bad.

Keeley put her head down on the table. She was starting to feel afraid, and she didn't like it. Beside her, the woman stopped sitting like a frozen ghost and started crying. Keeley didn't like that, either. She began to wish she had stayed home.

"Here you are." Keeley felt a familiar arm slide around her shoulders and smelled flowers in the air. She raised her head to see Violet smiling at her. "Of course, you would go wandering."

Violet looked over at the woman beside Keeley. "Let's get you both back to the boarding house. She'll be more comfortable there, and you can put some warm clothes on."

Keeley stood up, still pressing the bar towel against her head. Violet took one arm of the crying woman, Keeley took the other, and they left the saloon.

The nighttime darkness had begun to slip away. There were more people on the main street. A crowd had gathered at the end of Dominion Street, near the boarding house.

Dust still swirled in the air around them like a thick fog, and the early morning light was weak, but the people of Frank could still see what had happened.

The mountain had fallen on their town.

CHAPTER N° 4

For a long moment, no one spoke, and no one moved. Then the wailing started, rising up from everyone gathered there, as they began to understand the meaning of what had happened.

"Pop!" Keeley yelled. "Pop is in the mountain!"

She ran toward the rock slide. She had to get to Pop! She had to get the rocks out of the way so that Pop could get to her!

Nothing looked the way it should. Keeley couldn't get her bearings. The wall of boulders was in her way. It was a river of rocks, overflowing its banks.

She started to push against one of the boulders. It was as big as a house. She pushed and she pushed, hurling her weight against it until her hands and her face were scraped from the jagged edges of the granite. She pushed with everything she had in her, but the boulder would not move.

Keeley felt herself being lifted up. She couldn't fight the rock, so she fought the man who lifted her. He was strong and wrapped his arms around her until the fight was gone.

Keeley was surrounded by voices that talked to her softly and by a blanket that someone put over her shoulders. She started to cry. The man carried her gently back to the boarding house. She could tell she was put into Violet's bed by the scent of flowers all around.

Keeley kept her eyes shut. She didn't want to see what she knew she would see if she opened them up.

"I'll stay with her," she heard Violet say. Then everything was quiet. She felt Violet's hands brushing her hair off her face, and she fell into a deep, black sleep.

Violet was still with Keeley when she woke up with a start. For a moment, she was confused, and then everything came rushing back. "How long have I been asleep?"

"Almost an hour," Violet said. "You've had a terrible shock. How do you feel now?"

"I don't know."

Mrs. Greer came into the room with a basin of hot water.

"What do we do now?" Keeley asked.

"We'll get you cleaned up, then you'll stay in bed and out of the way," Mrs. Greer replied, wiping Keeley's face with a warm, wet cloth. Keeley saw the blood that had dried there from her battle with the boulder and from the cut on her head. Her face must look awful. It couldn't matter less.

"How bad is it outside?" Violet asked.

"News is trickling in. Looks like many of the cottages are buried and some of the tents, too,"

Mrs. Greer told her. "Rocks have dammed up the Oldman River, so there's been some flooding. Search and rescue parties are being organized, for the town and the mine."

"I have to help," Keeley said, waving away Mrs. Greer's washcloth.

"You have to do what you're told for once and not make any more trouble," Mrs. Greer snapped. "The best way you can help your father is to stay safe and let the rescuers look for him."

For a moment, Keeley was reassured. Mrs. Greer disapproving of her was normal. Maybe everything was going to be all right.

That hope disappeared with the next thing Mrs. Greer said.

"It looks like poor Lillian lost her whole family." Mrs. Greer finished wiping the blood off Keeley's hands and face, examined the scrapes, and decided they were not serious. The cut on Keeley's head wasn't deep, and it had stopped bleeding. "Their house was in the pathway of the rock slide. If Lillian hadn't slept here last night, she'd be gone, too." Mrs. Greer's breath caught as her emotions came into her voice.

She picked up the basin and headed to the door. "We can use your help in the kitchen," she said to Violet. "Those search parties will have to be fed."

"I'll be right down," Violet said.

"And you," Mrs. Greer said to Keeley, "stay in bed. We don't need any extra trouble today." She closed the door behind her.

"I agree with Mrs. Greer," Violet said. "The town won't be able to spare anyone to rescue you from whatever you get into."

Violet got her plainest dress out of the wardrobe and went behind her dressing screen to change out of her nightgown.

I can't stay in bed, Keeley thought. *I can't stay safe in here while my father is in trouble.*

She got up and headed on tiptoe out of Violet's room.

"Keeley," Violet began. Keeley stopped. "Dress warmly. And be careful."

"I will," Keeley promised. She went up to her room on the top floor. Lillian was face down on Pop's bed. Keeley didn't know what to say to her, so she said nothing as she put warm clothes on and headed back out into the wounded town.

CHAPTER N_o 5

The street in front of the boarding house was full of people getting themselves organized. Women on kitchen duty poured hot coffee into mugs that were passed around. Men and women with shovels and pickaxes grabbed sandwiches off trays before heading out toward the rock slide.

Keeley watched it all from the porch until she heard Mrs. Greer's voice from inside the boarding house. "Keep that coffee hot," Mrs. Greer said. Keeley slipped off the porch and through the crowd before she could be spotted and sent back to bed.

No one paid any attention to her. There were more important things for them to worry about. She heard bits of conversation as she headed toward the rocks.

"It's a miracle the train wasn't buried," someone said.

"The miners living in the tents—we'll never get them out," someone else said.

Panic rose again in Keeley's throat, but she fought it back. *This is just another bad day,* she told herself. *Soon I'll see my father and everyone else will turn up and everything will go back to normal.*

She tried very hard to believe that.

Keeley got to the end of the street, to where the mountain had slid. All she could see were rocks. Big ones.

"Come up here!" a voice above her said. Adam and Marcus, two boys she knew from school, were standing on the flat roof of the dress shop. "There's a ladder around the back."

Keeley had to climb over some of the rocks

to get behind the shop. She scrambled up the ladder. Adam helped pull her onto the roof.

"The whole mountain came down," Marcus said.

"Not the whole mountain. Look."

Keeley looked up at Turtle Mountain. The whole side of it was missing. Where once there had been deep green from countless fir trees, now there was bare rock. It was stark, it was bare, and it was ugly. Keeley turned away. She couldn't stand to look at it.

What she saw in the other direction was no more comforting. A field of rocks, of boulders, covered the valley and went partway up the mountain on the other side. The rocks covered the trees. They covered everything with their cold, hard ugliness.

It was the most horrible thing Keeley had ever seen.

"I was knocked out of my bed," Adam said.

"Everyone was," Marcus told him. "You're not special."

Keeley forced herself to look back up at the wounded mountain, but only as far up as the mine entrance should be.

There were only rocks.

"I've got to find my father," she said. "He's in the mine."

"You'll need a giant hammer to break through those rocks," Adam said, which led to a discussion between the two boys about just how big a hammer would be needed and how big a person would have to be to be able to swing such a hammer.

Idiots, thought Keeley. Without waiting to see how the argument ended, Keeley went back down the ladder.

She didn't know anyone with a giant hammer, but she did know someone with a big axe.

Granny Ethel would help her rescue her father.

Keeley headed back behind the main street to the meadow she had to cross on the way to Patricia's house. People were running from one place to another, some crying, some calling out names of family members who were missing. Others had armloads of blankets and offered them to people who had left their homes without coats.

Halfway across the meadow, Keeley felt the ground start to shake again. The people around her froze in place, like statues, looking up at Turtle Mountain.

Keeley saw something move at the top of the mountain. A huge slab of rock seemed to hover a moment in the air, then it rushed down in a cloud of stones and dust, making a roar like thunder. One woman screamed.

Is the whole mountain going to fall on us? Keeley wondered. Should she run? Could she outrun a mountain?

Keeley and the others didn't move. They watched the rock slab fall and break up into smaller pieces, with dust rising in a cloud at the bottom of the mountain. The roar stopped, the dust settled, and the mountain grew quiet once more.

The others in the meadow started moving again.

"False alarm," a man said to Keeley, looking much relieved. "I expect we'll see a few more of those before the mountain is finished."

Keeley wanted to ask him how he knew that, and what else he knew, but he was moving fast, and she needed to go in the other direction. Maybe he didn't really know anything. Maybe he was just talking, the way women did when they met in the streets and men did when they sat around in the tavern or the general store.

If anyone knew anything, it would be Granny Ethel.

The rocks had spilled across the meadow, and Keeley had to watch to make sure she didn't stumble over them as she ran. The boulders were bigger close to the treeline. A horrible fear entered Keeley's chest. What if Patricia's house was buried under rocks?

Maybe they're all in the tree house, she thought. She ran faster, trying to outrun her fear. She tried to hold that picture in her head: chaos down below but Patricia, Mable, and Ethel above it all in the tree house that had faces carved into the walls. Patricia would be reading, Granny Ethel would be sharpening her axe, and Granny Mable would be cutting slices of honey cake.

This comforting picture lasted until Keeley reached old Andy Grissick's campsite. Part of his tent stuck out from beneath a boulder.

"Mr. Grissick! Mr. Grissick! Are you all right?" Keeley rushed to the still-smouldering firepit, looking for the old trapper. She saw his frying pan leaning to one side of the pit. She bent down to pick it up and then backed away. She screamed and screamed.

The trapper's weather-gnarled hand was still clutching the frying pan's handle. The rest of him was under a boulder.

Keeley could do nothing but scream.

"It's all right," a soothing voice behind her said. "We're here."

Keeley spun around and was swooped up in Granny Ethel's arms. Granny Ethel, as solid as a mountain and more dependable, dropped her axe to the ground so she could sweep up Keeley with both arms. Patricia and Mable joined in the hug.

"We're all right," Ethel said. "Our house wasn't hit."

"Some of Ethel's sculptures are gone," Mable said, "and my bees were scared."

"Your bees will calm down, and I'll make more sculptures," Ethel said, placing Keeley back down on the ground. "We're heading into town to see how we can help."

"Mr. Grissick …," Keeley began.

"He's past our help," Ethel said. "Let's see to the living."

"We were halfway to town when we heard you screeching," Patricia said. Her arms were full of toys and books to give to children who had lost their homes. "You were wailing like a banshee."

"What's a banshee?" Keeley asked.

"You should read more," Patricia told her.

It was a wonderfully normal thing for her friend to say, and Keeley loved her for it. They all started walking back toward the town.

"My father is trapped in the mine," Keeley said. "I was coming to get you so you could help get him out."

"Ethel is going to join a rescue team," Mable said. "I'll help out the nurses. Patricia will look after any little ones who need to be looked after while their mothers are busy."

They reached the town. They stood at the end of the road and looked out at the acres of town and forest, now covered by rocks.

"I couldn't have imagined," Mable began, then she and Patricia hurried off to make themselves useful.

"Can we do it?" Keeley asked. "I mean, how can we?"

Ethel took a deep breath. "Do you know how the Italian artist Michelangelo carved his famous statue of David?"

Keeley shook her head.

"He took a good look at a piece of marble, and then he cut away all the parts that were not David. We'll do the same. We'll cut away all the parts of this that are not the town of Frank."

She swung her axe up on her shoulder. "But first, we'll go find your father."

The rescue party in charge of digging out the trapped miners was working on making a hole in the rocks.

"We think this is close to where they were working," one of the men said, as he paused to catch his breath. "We hope, anyway." He swung his pickaxe again.

Granny Ethel joined in, using her axe like a shovel and a crowbar, and heaving huge rocks out of the way with her powerful arms. Keeley was too small to be useful digging. She fetched coffee, cider, water, and sandwiches from town. When the diggers' hands became blistered, she volunteered to go find work gloves. There were no gloves left in town—they were all being used by other rescue teams—but Keeley got an old bed sheet from Mrs. Greer, who was not surprised to see her out of bed. Keeley tore this into strips of cloth for the men and Ethel to wrap around their hands for protection.

Every now and then, the mountain would rumble again and shower more rocks down around them. Keeley got hit in the arm with one but didn't complain. It didn't hurt too badly, and she didn't want the digging to stop for anything.

"I need some more coffee," one of the men said, stretching his back to give it some relief. "What in the world is that?"

They all followed his gaze.

A child wandered among the rocks, all alone, nightclothes hanging off him in rags. His face and his front were crimson with blood.

"Oh, my goodness, it's Peter!" Keeley realized.

Ethel got to him first. "Peter, what happened to you?"

Peter was too dazed to speak.

"He's got feathers sticking out of him," Keeley said. Blood stuck to his skin and what remained of his pyjamas.

"We'll get him to the hospital." Two men tossed down their shovels, covered Peter with one of their coats, made a chair of their hands, and gently carried him down to slope toward the remains of the town.

Don't stop digging! Keeley wanted to yell, but she also wanted Peter to be looked after. She looked back and forth between the abandoned shovels and her injured classmate, unsure of what to do.

"Go down there with Peter," Granny Ethel told her. "Make sure there are people there who know him and will look out for his family. And bring back some more food."

Keeley grabbed the empty baskets and ran after Peter, glad to have something useful to do.

Strangers had come from other communities in the Crowsnest Pass to help out. Peter was received into the makeshift hospital by people Keeley didn't know. She told a nurse his name and where they found him.

"It looks like the force of the rocks falling pushed his featherbed right inside him," the nurse said. "It's a miracle he was able to walk." She tried to usher Keeley out, but Keeley couldn't leave Peter just like that.

"I'll beat you at next year's spelling bee," she told him. What she meant was, there *will* be a next year and we'll hate each other as much as ever and everything will be fine and back to normal. But Peter had passed out, and she didn't think he heard her.

The mountain had slid over the miners' camp, burying men in their tents and whole families in their homes. Most of the men and women in the town who were able were already part of rescue teams. There weren't many people left who could go look for Peter's parents.

"There are already people digging over there," Mrs. Greer said when Keeley appealed to her. She was sitting in a quiet corner with Lillian. Lillian looked all cried out, and Mrs. Greer looked tired. "Peter's house is on a street where a lot of houses were hit."

"I have to be sure," Keeley said and ran off down the street. The saloon was always full of men. Some of them would not be too drunk to help her.

She was almost there when the cheers began.

"The miners are out! The miners are out!"

Keeley ran back. On Dominion Street, a crowd had gathered. Down the centre of the road came seventeen miners, some walking and leaning on each other, some wounded and riding in a cart.

"They dug themselves out just a few yards from where we'd been digging to go in after them," she heard one of the rescuers say. "I don't know how they did it."

Keeley jumped in the cart, putting her face close to the dust-covered and bandaged faces. "Pop? Pop?"

She ran among the walking miners. "Pop! Pop!"

The last miner in the line grabbed her by the shoulders. He squatted down to look her in the eye.

"Your father was having his lunch at the mine entrance," the miner said. "We haven't seen him since the rock slide. He isn't with us."

Keeley sat down in the road and cried. She wasn't the only one. She heard one of the miners close by sobbing after someone told him his whole family was dead.

Granny Ethel had joined the crowd. She lifted Keeley and carried her to Violet's bed in the boarding house. This time, Keeley stayed there.

CHAPTER N.º 7

"*As your premier, I have taken it upon*
myself to consult with expert geologists."
Premier Haultain made a speech to the townspeople, the day after the miners were rescued.
Keeley stood with the others, gathered in the
same spot where the town's founding picnic had
taken place, only one and a half years before.

"They need to make a more detailed study of
Turtle Mountain, but they tell me there is a real
danger of another major rock slide. For this
reason, I am ordering the immediate evacuation
of the town of Frank."

This news caused barely a murmur among the people around Keeley. They had been expecting it. Many people had left already.

"Trains have been made available to take you to Blairmore, where temporary accommodation has been set up for those who do not have another place to go. Inspector Primrose of the North-West Mounted Police and his men will patrol the town, along with Constable Leard, to ensure that your property is safe from looting."

A man in a police uniform stood up to speak. "I am Inspector Primrose," he said. "This evacuation order is mandatory. Anyone refusing to leave will be put onto the train by force. Anyone caught in town without permission will be arrested."

"What if I don't want to go?" Keeley asked later, as she packed her things into a bundle. Violet helped her by folding the clothing.

"We're not being asked," was Mrs. Greer's reply. She was helping Lillian pack. All Lillian had of her own was what she was wearing the day before the rock slide. Everything else was buried in her house, along with her family. Mrs. Greer and the other ladies in the boarding house had given her some of their clothes. She was still using Keeley's father's bed.

"You should be going off to your grandparents' anyway," Mrs. Greer said. "There's nothing you can do here."

Keeley knew that Mrs. Greer also wanted to say, "There's rent due on your room, and you are not my responsibility." She was grateful to Mrs. Greer for not saying it.

"Do I take everything?" she asked, looking around at her mother's paintings on the walls. Keeley's grandparents hadn't liked the paintings. If she lived with them, her mother's work would once again be wrapped up tight and hidden away. Keeley's heart grew very heavy.

"The paintings will be safer with you," Violet said. "I'll pack them for you."

"Hurry up," Mrs. Greer said. "The premier said we were to hurry." Mrs. Greer touched the sloping wall of the upper room and sighed deeply. Keeley saw that her landlady was trying not to cry. She understood. Mrs. Greer was leaving everything behind, too. At least Keeley could wrap up her mother's paintings and carry them with her. The boarding house would have to stay behind.

Keeley and Lillian walked behind the adults as they joined the long line of townspeople heading out of Frank, taking with them only what they could carry. Keeley had her mother's paintings in one bundle and her and her father's clothes in another.

"What will you do?" Keeley asked Lillian.

"Mrs. Greer said she'd keep me on, and I could live at the boarding house. Now, who knows? Get a job somewhere, I suppose."

She sounded so lonely. Keeley couldn't think of anything to say to make her feel better, so she said nothing.

There hadn't been time after the evacuation order to go find Patricia. Keeley kept her eyes open for her friends, but there were so many people around, she couldn't see them.

The people of Frank walked a mile down a forest path to the North-West Mounted Police outpost. The police barracks had already been turned into a temporary hospital for the wounded who were not yet well enough to travel. Keeley thought about going in to say goodbye to Peter, but she didn't. For some reason, the thought of never seeing him again made her feel far too sad.

The train was waiting for them. Police officers and town officials helped people climb on board. Keeley thought she saw Granny Ethel getting into the next train car. She started to jump up and down and yell to get her attention.

"You'll see her when the train stops," a familiar voice said. Her teacher, Miss Griffin, was right behind her. She pushed Keeley onto the train car steps.

"You don't get to boss me around outside the classroom!"

An astonished silence followed, with no one more astonished than Keeley. Had she really spoken such rudeness out loud?

"It's all right, Keeley. Everything will be OK." Miss Griffin spoke in a soothing, gentle voice, one that Keeley had never heard from her teacher before.

Then she understood. Miss Griffin thought Keeley was an orphan. Miss Griffin felt sorry for her.

She pulled herself away and tried to get back down the train car steps, but the crush of people was too tight. She was swept along with them farther into the car.

There were not enough places for everyone to sit. Keeley had to stand in the aisle, just as she had done when she first came to Frank, on the town's founding day.

Her father had been with her then. She swallowed hard to keep from crying. She had nothing left now.

"They've allowed Harry Matheson to stay,"

Keeley heard someone say. "Don't know why he's bothering to put a newspaper out. No one's left in town to read it."

Mr. Matheson was staying? Keeley still had one thing left. She was going to be a reporter, and reporters belonged where the story was happening, not crushed into a train being taken away.

"Let me out!" she shouted, pushing her way through the crowd with a force that got stronger as the train started moving. Keeley showed no grace and gave no apology as she thrust, elbowed, and shoved her way to the door. Miss Griffin was blocking her way.

"Keeley, I forbid ..."

Keeley never knew what it was her teacher was forbidding. She pushed Miss Griffin out of the way with a mighty shove and jumped through the open train door. She tumbled down a small hill until she hit a tree and stopped.

Nothing was broken. She stood up and watched the rest of the train pass by. It gathered speed and was soon just a puff of steam in the distance.

It was then that Keeley was hit with a wave of grief so strong she dropped to the ground.

Somehow, she'd left her mother's paintings on the train.

CHAPTER *N*^o 8

Keeley picked up her remaining bundl
and headed back down the path. She heard voices
remembered the inspector's threat to arrest anyon
caught in town without permission, and ducked
quickly into the trees. Crouching behind some
fallen logs, she waited until the policemen passed
by her on their way into town before getting up
again. She kept to the woods and kept her eyes
open, sneaking up on the town.

She'd gotten some practice during her time
in Frank at being in places where she wasn't
supposed to be. It had felt like a game then.

The town looked sad without its people. The chickens and goats some folks kept in their yards would need feeding. She could take on that chore. That would prove she was responsible enough to stay.

Keeley peered out of an alleyway into the main street. She'd have to walk out there to get to the newspaper office. Quickly, she pulled her head back in. Inspector Primrose was coming! She backed into a corner and pulled some crates in front of her.

Inspector Primrose met one of his officers at the end of Keeley's alley. They started a conversation. Keeley's legs were in an awkward position, and they started to cramp. Why did adults talk so much?

Keeley heard a sniffling noise, then a little growl.

Dexter, the terrier belonging to the Welsh miners who lived next to the stable, had found her.

"Go away," she whispered, which did no good at all. She grabbed a nearby bit of board and tossed it. Dexter went after it but was soon back again, the board in his mouth, his tail wagging.

Keeley peered out at the two policemen. They were still yakking. She reached out, grabbed Dexter, and pulled him into her hiding place with one smooth motion. He wiggled and kissed her, his nub of a tail wagging so furiously, Keeley had to tuck his whole little body into her coat to avoid them both being discovered.

Finally, the two men ran out of words and walked away. Keeley released Dexter, checked the street, and hurried into the newspaper office.

Mr. Matheson was at the rows of type letters, composing an article. Keeley slipped onto her stool, picked up one of the articles he had ready, and started checking it for spelling mistakes.

All was quiet for a moment and then Mr. Matheson said, "Did you think I wouldn't notice?" He sat down beside her. "It's not safe for you here."

"It's not safe for you either, but here you are. Besides, I can't leave until I know for sure about my father. He still has a chance."

Mr. Matheson rubbed his face, smearing ink on his forehead. "I can't look after you."

"I'll look after myself. If I get in your way, you can turn me over to the police." She kept looking at the news article. She could feel Mr. Matheson staring at her and thinking.

"Do you think you can actually do as you're told?"

"As long as I'm not told to do anything stupid like get on a train when my life is here." She looked him straight in the eye.

Mr. Matheson laughed at that. "Your life is not here, Keeley O'Brien. Your life needs a much bigger world than Frank can offer you. But all right, I'll square things with the constable. You can sleep on a mat beside the printing press."

He got off the stool and came back with some paper and a pencil. "Leave that proof-reading for now. I want you to write down everything you remember since the rock slide. I want you to write down whatever you see or hear over the next few days. We're a part of Canadian history now." He went back to his rows of type.

Keeley peered out at the two policemen. They were still yakking. She reached out, grabbed Dexter, and pulled him into her hiding place with one smooth motion.

"Will you print my story in the paper? Does this mean I'm a reporter now?"

"You can't write and ask questions at the same time," was her editor's reply.

For the next few days, Keeley was kept so busy, she didn't have time to worry about her father, her friends, her mother's paintings, or anything other than her work.

"Go out into the street and write down what you see," Mr. Matheson would bark at her. "Put the date and time at the top of the page. Remember the five questions."

"Who, what, when, where, and why," Keeley would reply. The "why" was the only one she could never answer.

The police allowed her to feed the animals left behind. "One less job for us," she was told.

Dexter went everywhere with her. She had a feeling his owners weren't coming back.

"The floor needs sweeping. Make fresh coffee. Bring some firewood in." Keeley was glad of the activity. When it stopped, she thought about her father, up on the mountain, under the rocks. It made her want to scream.

"Proofread this," her editor would tell her. "Go ask the mayor if that geologist has anything to say yet."

As a newspaper woman, Keeley didn't have to be in awe of the mayor or Inspector Primrose.

"They're public servants," Mr. Matheson said. "They work for us. It's our job to keep track of what they're up to."

"Who do we work for?" Keeley asked.

"The public," was her editor's reply. Keeley liked that. It made her feel important. Her father would be impressed.

Every day, she hiked over to the makeshift hospital in the police headquarters and saw Peter. His family had been able to crawl away from the wreckage of their house and were staying near him in the hospital. For the first two days, he smiled weakly at Keeley when she talked to him. On the third day, he told her that her hair looked like a witch's, and Keeley knew he was feeling better.

Time went by quickly. Keeley ate hunks of bread and salami when she was hungry and went to sleep when she was too tired to stay awake. It was an adventure, living a grown-up life, and it would have been fun if it weren't for the pit of cold loneliness she carried around with her.

Finally, the geologist had something to say. "The mountain is safe," he announced. "People can come back to the town."

Mr. Matheson wrote the story and Keeley checked it for spelling mistakes. Other papers in Lethbridge, Calgary, and Blairmore printed the news, too, and people started coming back into town.

"Can you give me a real job?" Keeley asked her editor. "Can I stay on here full time? You can see that I'm a good worker. Let me work here all the time."

"The school will soon reopen," Mr. Matheson said. "That's where you belong. And you can't keep sleeping in the newsroom. You should go back to the boarding house."

"How can I stay in Frank if I don't have enough money?" Mrs. Greer would want rent. "Why won't you give me a full-time job?"

"Because your father wouldn't want me to," he said. Keeley knew Mr. Matheson wouldn't change his mind.

She went back to the boarding house. Violet and Mrs. Greer were glad to see her. "Thank you for taking care of the animals," Mrs. Greer said.

Keeley went up to her old room at the top of the house. Lillian had already unpacked and was taking a nap on Pop's bed.

Keeley put down her bundle. She pulled the curtains across the window so she wouldn't have to look at the mountain and wondered how long she'd be allowed to stay, and why she even wanted to.

CHAPTER N° 9

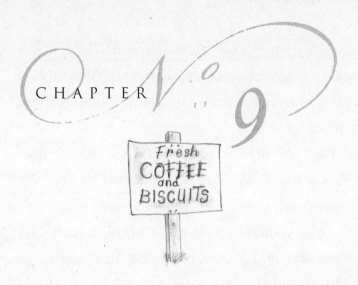

Patricia and her grandmothers were in the first wave of people who returned to Frank.

"We heard you jumped off the train," Patricia said. "How exciting! Just like a prison break!" She waved her current book, *The Count of Monte Cristo,* under Keeley's nose. "Peter will be jealous when he finds out. Is he all right?"

"He's well enough to be annoying," Keeley said. "His parents are taking him to Blairmore tomorrow. They're not going to stay in Frank."

"I think jumping out of a moving train is better than winning a spelling bee," Patricia said, which is one of the reasons Keeley was glad to have her as a best friend. Although it was a lifetime since a spelling bee seemed important.

Parts of life in Frank returned to normal. People still needed to eat, so the general store, the restaurants, and the saloons opened up.

They didn't have many customers that first week, though. People were slow to come back. Some refused. Keeley heard reports of people who were simply too scared or who had nothing left to come back to.

The diggers went back to work at the mine entrance the moment they were told they could come back. The ones who came from out of town took rooms at the boarding house.

"Is the town finished?" Keeley asked them at supper. "Will people come back?" She handed them a tray of boiled cabbage she'd fetched from the kitchen. She was trying to make herself as useful as possible, hoping Mrs. Greer would forget about asking for the rent.

"There's still coal in the mountain," the digger said. "Canada needs coal more than ever. We'll know more once we get to the entrance."

"Are you getting closer?"

"Closer every day."

Nobody told Keeley her father was all right. Nobody told her he was dead. Strange things happened in mines. No one placed any bets one way or another.

Violet came back a few days later. The boarding house smelled of flowers again. She and Keeley spent their evenings together, playing card games with some of the other boarders in Mrs. Greer's big kitchen. They helped each other feel less lonely.

Keeley spent her time doing chores for Mrs. Greer, and she was better at them than she expected to be. All those times of doing chores for punishment had taught her something.

She also ran errands for Mr. Matheson and checked his articles for spelling mistakes. She continued caring for the animals of people who hadn't returned yet.

Whenever she was free, she took coffee, water, and sandwiches up to the diggers.

We're coming for you, Pop, she'd say in her mind. Every day, they got a little closer.

After a week had passed and no more rocks had fallen from the mountain, people who had been scared to return began to come back, and the town became lively again.

The premier came back to town, along with the mayors and people from around the Crowsnest Pass. A memorial service was held for all the people who had been killed in the mountain slide. The halls of the town were too small to hold all the people who came. They had to hold the service outside.

"We would like you to sit up front with the rest of the mourners," the pastor said to Keeley before the service. "You will want to be there when we read out the name of your father."

"My father is not dead," Keeley said. "He's missing. They're looking for him."

"Would you like to talk about it, my child?"

What I would like to do is kick you, Keeley thought, but she didn't. Kicking a pastor was sure to be worse than pushing a teacher.

"Leave her father's name off the list," Mrs. Greer said. Not even the pastor would dare to argue with Mrs. Greer.

"We don't know all their names," the premier said. "Frank was growing so quickly, not everyone had a chance to make themselves known. I'm told some of the men who died had arrived in Frank just a few days before, eager to make their fortunes in coal. We mourn them as much as we mourn those who were well known."

Most of the dead were still buried under tons of rock. The only way to get their bodies out would be to use dynamite to blast them out. The feeling in the town was to let the dead rest. They and their families had been through enough.

Keeley helped pass around sandwiches at the social gathering after the service.

"We pay that teacher darn good money," an old woman said to another, as they balanced their tea cups and snacks. "She should be back here by now. All these children are running wild."

"You don't pay her good money—you pay her almost nothing," Keeley said. "And we are not running wild."

"Young lady, do you mean to tell us Miss Griffin discussed her salary with her students?"

"Of course not," Keeley replied. "Her salary is on record at the town hall. You pay her less than they pay the man who looks after the mine horses."

"How dare you speak to us like this! And how dare you go snooping around the town hall!"

"I wasn't snooping. I'm a citizen. I have a right to know." Keeley whisked away the plate of sandwiches just as one of the ladies was reaching for one.

She was back in the kitchen before she wondered why she had stuck up for Miss Griffin. She surprised herself even more by feeling sorry she'd had to shove her teacher so hard on the train.

The following Saturday, the streets were suddenly full of people.

"Tourists!" Mrs. Greer said. "Come to see the rock slide! Who could have guessed?"

She ran to put more coffee on. Lillian was put to work making biscuits. Keeley was sent to the basement for jars of rhubarb and raspberry preserves. By the time she came back up again, there was a sign on Mrs. Greer's front lawn: "Fresh Coffee and Biscuits."

The rock slide had hurt people's businesses. The tourists were a chance to make back some of the money the town had lost. Instantly, it seemed to Keeley, there were guided tours of the slide, folks could have their photographs taken beside the giant boulders, and a new confection called Turtle Mountain Rock Candy was being sold on the street corners.

And Violet lost her job in the saloon.

"They wanted me to be happy," she told Keeley that night. "They said, 'What good is a dance hall girl who is not cheerful?' I suppose they're right. But I miss your father too much! Customers complained that all I talked about was what a wonderful man your father is. The boss said I was bad for business, and he fired me."

Violet cried. Keeley fetched her tea and sat with her and helped her get through the night. Being with someone who loved her father as much as she did made her feel better.

They didn't talk about the future. There was nothing they could say.

CHAPTER N° 10

"They've broken through the mine! They've found a survivor!"

The shouts reached Keeley where she was turning over the soil in Mrs. Greer's backyard kitchen garden, to get it ready for planting. She dropped the pitchfork and ran.

Her legs moved so fast, she wasn't even sure her feet were touching the ground, but she pumped them even harder. She ran too fast to think. She just knew she had to get there.

A crowd had already formed.

The mine entrance was open. It wasn't as big

as it usually was, and it would have to be shored up again with new timber, but it was there.

"Pop!" she yelled. It came out as a croak, without enough breath behind it. She panted a moment and then tried again. "Pop!"

She tried to get into the mine, but one of the diggers held her back.

"Stay out of the way," he said.

"They're coming!" someone shouted.

Keeley leaned forward, tears falling down her face. "Pop, Pop, oh, Pop," she chanted as she breathed.

A group of men pulled and pushed a cart through the last few yards of the mine. When they reached the entrance, Keeley could wait no longer. She ran toward them.

"Pop!" She threw herself at the cart.

But it wasn't Pop in the cart. It was Charlie, the mine horse.

There was a cheer from the crowd, as a man came forward with a bucket of beer for the horse to drink, and another man brought over hay and

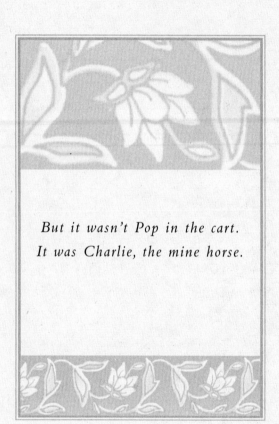

But it wasn't Pop in the cart.
It was Charlie, the mine horse.

oats. "Stupid people." One of the diggers came to stand beside Keeley. "That wonderful horse kept himself alive by licking water dripping in the mine shaft. And now these idiots are going to kill him by overfeeding him and giving him beer."

He knelt down beside Keeley. "We never found your father," he said. "He's not in the mine. They say he was having lunch outside when the rock slide hit. That means he's buried under these rocks. There's no place else he could be."

He could have run to the top of the mountain when the rocks started coming down, Keeley thought desperately. *He could be hidden in a secret room inside the mine, writing his poems and wondering if I'm staying out of trouble.*

"Could somebody stay with this little girl?" he called out.

"I'm all right," Keeley tried to say, but she was trembling all over.

Violet had heard the shouts and Mrs. Greer, too. They took Keeley back to the boarding house and sat with her in the parlour while she cried and cried. When Keeley couldn't cry any more, Mrs. Greer put on the kettle and made them all some tea.

They sat at the kitchen table. For a long time, no one spoke. Mrs. Greer finally broke the silence. "Keeley, I'm very sorry. I truly am. I liked your father a great deal. He was the kindest gentleman to ever stay at my boarding house."

"Thank you," said Keeley. "He'd have been glad to know that."

"Well, I told him so, and I'm glad I did. Keeley, I'm going to need the name and address of your grandparents."

"Is there no other way?" Violet asked.

"She's their granddaughter. They're her family."

Keeley remembered something. "I have five dollars in the bank, from when I won the spelling bee last year, and I saved some of the money I made at the newspaper this year. I could pay rent with that."

"That money won't last very long, and when it's gone, you'll be faced with the same problem, but without money in the bank." Mrs. Greer was firm. "You're too young to live alone but not too young to realize that. Now excuse me. I must go and write them a letter."

"Couldn't I stay here and work for you, like Lillian is doing?" Keeley heard the pleading in her voice, but this was her last chance. She couldn't go back to live with her grandparents in Lethbridge! Already she could feel the house with all its doilies and breakable things closing in around her.

"Lillian is nearly a grown woman, and you are a child. You should live somewhere where you can go to school—and your father would be the first one to tell you that." Mrs. Greer left the room and put an end to the discussion.

Violet took Keeley's hand. "I'll have to move on, too. I don't have a job. If I had some extra money, I could take you with me, but …"

"It's all right," Keeley said. She understood about needing money.

Word spreads fast in a small town. Patricia and

her grandmothers were at the boarding house within the hour.

"Pack your things," Granny Mable said. "You can live with us."

"We've always wanted another granddaughter," Ethel said. "Patricia doesn't cause us nearly enough trouble."

"Are you sure?" Keeley asked. "I can't pay much."

"We're family now," Mable said. "We'll work it out. You can help me with the bees."

Keeley would be happy to do anything.

"We're already best friends," Patricia said. "Now we'll be sisters."

It didn't take Keeley long to pack her things. She was glad to be leaving the little room at the top of the house. It made her sad.

She thought about sneaking away, in case there was rent owing, but that didn't seem right. She told Mrs. Greer she was leaving.

"If there's rent owing, I'd like to know, so I can pay it," Keeley said, "although I may not be able to pay it all right away."

"That's just how your father would have put it," Mrs. Greer said. "There's no rent owing."

"Since I'll be living with Mable and Ethel, you don't need to write to my grandparents," Keeley said.

"I just sent Lillian to post that letter," Mrs. Greer said. "You're their granddaughter. They have a right to know what's happening to you."

"I'll write them another letter," Keeley decided, "and tell them not to worry." She gave Mrs. Greer a hug.

"When the town gets back on its feet, and business is good again, come and see me," Mrs. Greer told her. "I may have little after-school jobs for you from time to time."

"I'll do that," Keeley promised.

Keeley was very glad she hadn't kicked the pastor, because she had to go see him about performing a memorial service for her father.

"Your father was a good man," he said. "We'll give him a good service."

Many people had liked her father, and they

came to the service. Keeley got up and talked about him, about the things he believed about the world, and about how much she would miss him. She read out one of his poems. She got through the whole service without crying.

With the mine open again, people flooded back into Frank. There were new houses to be built, to replace the ones destroyed by the slide, and there was lots of work for everyone.

Miss Griffin came back, too. Keeley didn't know her teacher was back in town until she and Patricia suddenly heard the school bell ringing. They had to interrupt their very important work of looking for tadpoles to run home, grab their books, and get to the school. They arrived late, and unwashed, but Miss Griffin was still happy to see them.

"I'm sorry I pushed you," Keeley said, hoping the quick apology would ward off any punishment. Also, she really was sorry.

"It's all right," Miss Griffin said, "and you must tell me all about your adventure—an essay about it by the end of the week would be nice—but first, I have something to tell you. I found your mother's paintings."

That was so unexpected. Keeley didn't know what to say.

"I didn't know if I'd ever see you again. I wasn't planning on coming back to Frank. I haven't been happy here, and the mountain slide gave me a good excuse to leave." Miss Griffin paused.

"Where are they?" Keeley asked.

"I gave them to a friend of mine who was on his way to Winnipeg. His friend runs an art gallery there." She handed Keeley a letter. "Your mother's paintings caused a lot of excitement. They'd like your permission to hang the paintings in their gallery. You still own them," she added quickly. "You'd just be loaning them to the gallery."

"How do I say yes?"

"After school, I'll take you to the telegraph office and you can send them a wire. They'll pay for it," she added.

People had loved Keeley's father, and now they

loved her mother's paintings. The world seemed a little kinder to Keeley that day.

A week after that, there was a celebration dinner with the grandmothers. Violet had just been taken on as a salesgirl at a new ladies' fancy dress shop on the main street.

"All the ladies in Frank will be as beautiful as you," Keeley said. She and Patricia toasted Violet with apple juice, the grown-ups with honey-wine.

"If Cleopatra were alive today, what sort of dress do you think she would like to wear?" Mable asked, which led to a wonderful discussion about beauty and fashion through the ages. They were laughing over picturing one another with Marie Antoinette hairdos when someone knocked at the door.

"I'll get it," Keeley said. Still laughing, she opened the door.

Mrs. Greer was there, looking truly sorry.

Behind her was Keeley's grandmother.

"Get your things, Keeley Lee," her grandmother said. "I'm taking you home."

CHAPTER № 11

"Just when things were starting to feel normal again." Keeley put the last of her things into her bag.

"She won't even let you stay here tonight!" Patricia complained. The train didn't leave until the next day. "She looked at us as though she could catch something nasty from us."

Keeley stuck her nose in the air, in a bad imitation of her grandmother. "I'm not leaving my granddaughter in the company of such ... women!"

"At least you'll get to spend a night in the

hotel. That will be fun, won't it?" Patricia was trying to find a bright side. "And Lethbridge isn't that far away. You could come and visit."

"My grandmother has a talent for taking the fun out of everything," Keeley said, "and she'll keep me locked up so tight in Lethbridge, I won't even be able to breathe if she decides it's unladylike."

"A girl who jumps off a moving train should be able to find a way," Patricia pointed out.

That gave Keeley some hope.

Saying goodbye was horrible.

"Don't think you're free of us," Mable said, when Mrs. Greer had taken Keeley's grand-mother out of earshot.

"We're going to keep in touch with you, and keep track of you, so you'd better do great things," Violet said. She pressed a handkerchief, loaded with scent from her perfume, into Keeley's hand.

Granny Ethel, the rock, the mountain, picked her up and held her close. "How you live is a choice," she said. "Never forget that. *You* decide. Don't let others decide for you." She put Keeley back down.

"We're still sisters, right?" Patricia said. "We'll always be sisters."

Keeley's night in the hotel was as un-fun as she predicted it would be. Her grandmother wouldn't let her eavesdrop in the lobby or watch people in the saloon or do any of the things that should be done on such an adventure.

"Don't look so glum," her grandmother said. "You're being given a good home where you'll receive a proper upbringing. Is that so terrible?"

"No, Grandmother." When it was put like that, Keeley really had no reason to feel sorry for herself. She was still sad though.

On their way to the train the next morning, they stopped at the bank. Keeley took her Spelling Bee winnings and the money she had saved from her job at the newspaper out of her savings account and closed it. She tucked the money into a pocket in her jacket.

"Do you want me to hold on to that money for you?" Grandmother asked.

"No, thank you. I've got it."

Mr. Matheson was waiting for them at the train. He introduced himself to Keeley's grandmother. "Keeley will make a fine newspaper reporter one day."

"Not a very suitable place for a lady," her grandmother said.

"Ladies are showing up in all sorts of places these days," Mr. Matheson said. "They'll even be in Parliament before long."

"All aboard," the conductor called out.

Mr. Matheson gave Keeley the newspaper he was carrying. "Page four," he said. "Keep in touch."

"Come, Keeley," her grandmother told her. Keeley shook hands with her editor and followed her grandmother to the train.

There were not enough seats. Her grandmother was able to sit, but Keeley had to stand in the aisle.

Will I ever get a seat on a train? she wondered.

Before the train started up, she unfolded the newspaper to page four. She scanned the headlines and then let out a whoop.

MY LIFE THROUGH THE ROCK SLIDE
By Keeley O'Brien

"He printed what I wrote! I've got an article in the newspaper! I'm a reporter! Look!" She stuck the article under her grandmother's nose.

Just then, the train started up. Keeley fell into her grandmother's lap and the lap of the woman next to her. By the time she got herself untangled and stood up, and the ladies straightened out their hats, nobody was in the mood to see Keeley's story. She tucked it into the bundle at her feet. She would read it later, to herself.

Lethbridge has a newspaper too, she thought. She'd show the editor her article. Maybe he'd give her a job.

A man on the other side of the aisle was reading a newspaper. Keeley leaned over to look at it, to see if it was the Lethbridge paper.

It wasn't. It was the Winnipeg newspaper.

Keeley thought about her mother's paintings, hanging in a gallery in Winnipeg. She sure would like to see them there. Touching the money in her pocket, she wondered if that was enough money for the fare.

She leaned in closer, reading over the man's shoulder. He was reading an article by Cora Hind, Keeley's reporter friend.

Cora Hind was in Winnipeg. Two reasons to go to Winnipeg; no reasons to go to Lethbridge.

Keeley made her decision.

She bent down to talk to her grandmother. She had to talk loudly to be heard over the train noises and other conversations.

"Grandmother, I want to tell you that I'm grateful for all you've done for me, for taking Pop and me in when Mama died and for taking me in now. I want to say thank you."

"Very nicely said, dear," her grandmother said, "but it's not polite to raise your voice in public."

Keeley really did love her grandmother at that moment. Bending down farther, she kissed her on the cheek. She saw the old woman allow herself a brief smile.

Keeley dropped her voice to a whisper. "And I'm sorry for all the trouble I'm about to cause you."

The Lethbridge train station was a busy place. It would be easy to slip away and find the train to Winnipeg.

Keeley rocked back and forth with the rhythm of the train. In her head, she began to make plans.

Author's Note

On April 29, 1903, a huge chunk of rock broke off from the top of Turtle Mountain and slid down onto the town of Frank below. Part of the town was, and still is, buried under tons of granite. Approximately seventy people died that day.

There are several reasons why the slide happened. The coal was taken out of the mountain very quickly, which changed the shape of the mountain, making a weak point in the rock even weaker. Very warm weather that April melted the winter snow, and the sudden, drastic drop in temperature that followed froze all the water trickling through the mountain. This extra stress on the rock was enough to cause the rock slide.

There still is a town of Frank, Alberta, across the highway from the original town. The rock slide is still there and deep underneath it, the seventy people whose lives were lost.

ACKNOWLEDGEMENTS

I would like to express my thanks to the folks at the

Frank Slide Interpretive Centre in Frank, Alberta,

for their assistance with this book.

Dear Reader,

*Welcome back to Our Canadian Girl!
In addition to this story about Keeley,
there are many more adventures of other
spirited girls to come.*

*So please keep on reading. And do stay
in touch. You can also log on to our website
at www.ourcanadiangirl.ca and enjoy fun
activities, sample chapters, a fan club, and
monthly contests.*

*Sincerely,
Barbara Berson
Editor*

1608
Samuel de Champlain establishes the first fortified trading post at Quebec.

1759
The British defeat the French in the Battle of the Plains of Abraham.

1812
The United States declares war against Canada.

1845
The expedition of Sir John Franklin to the Arctic ends when the ship is frozen in the pack ice; the fate of its crew remains a mystery.

1869
Louis Riel leads his Métis followers in the Red River Rebellion.

1871
British Columbia joins Canada.

1755
The British expel the entire French population of Acadia (today's Maritime provinces), sending them into exile.

1776
The 13 Colonies revolt against Britain, and the Loyalists flee to Canada.

1837
Calling for responsible government, the Patriotes, following Louis-Joseph Papineau, rebel in Lower Canada; William Lyon Mackenzie leads the uprising in Upper Canada.

1867
New Brunswick, Nova Scotia and the United Province of Canada come together in Confederation to form the Dominion of Canada.

1870
Manitoba joins Canada. The Northwest Territories become an official territory of Canada.

1784
Rachel

Timeline

1885
At Craigellachie, British Columbia, the last spike is driven to complete the building of the Canadian Pacific Railway.

1898
The Yukon Territory becomes an official territory of Canada.

1914
Britain declares war on Germany, and Canada, because of its ties to Britain, is at war too.

1918
As a result of the Wartime Elections Act, the women of Canada are given the right to vote in federal elections.

1945
World War II ends conclusively with the dropping of atomic bombs on Hiroshima and Nagasaki.

1873
Prince Edward Island joins Canada.

1896
Gold is discovered on Bonanza Creek, a tributary of the Klondike River.

1905
Alberta and Saskatchewan join Canada.

1917
In the Halifax harbour, two ships collide, causing an explosion that leaves more than 1,600 dead and 9,000 injured.

1939
Canada declares war on Germany seven days after war is declared by Britain and France.

1949
Newfoundland, under the leadership of Joey Smallwood, joins Canada.

1885
Marie-Claire

1903
Keeley

1914
Millie

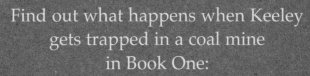
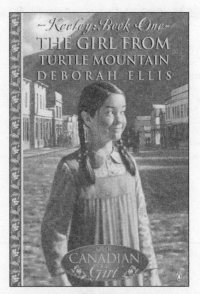

Meet Angelique
in Book One:
Buffalo Hunt

In 1865, Angelique is caught amidst a buffalo stampede in her first hunt alongside the adults.

Also available:
Angelique, Book Two: *The Long Way Home* and
Angelique, Book Three: *Autumn Alone*

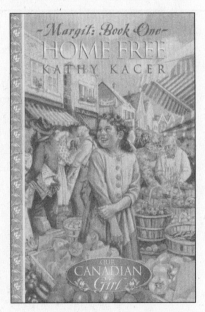

Meet all the
Our Canadian Girls!

Learn more about these strong, smart,
and courageous girls by visiting
www.ourcanadiangirl.ca